ESCAPE

NITTY GRITTY NOVELS

GLYNNE MacLEAN

ESCAPE

www.pearsoned.co.nz

Your comments on this title are welcome at
feedback@pearsoned.co.nz

Pearson
a division of Pearson New Zealand Ltd
67 Apollo Drive, Rosedale, Auckland 0632, New Zealand

Associated companies throughout the world

Escape

Story by Glynne MacLean

U.S. edition by Houghton Mifflin Harcourt Publishing Company

Printed in China via Pearson Education Asia (EPC/01)

ISBN 978-0-5479-8602-9

10 9 8 7 6   1846   12 11 10
4500000000   A B C D E F G

AUTHOR NOTE

The island of Socotra captured my imagination the first time I saw pictures of it. It has a wild, varied landscape and exotic bird and plant life. Socotra is the home of the weird dragon's blood tree and the frankincense tree.

For centuries, Socotra was a vital point on major trade routes. As long as trade goods were transported on the oceans, traders and sailors visited Socotra from near and far, and Socotra was important. Pirates were frequent visitors, too.

When I was thinking about Socotra, I was also thinking about friends. I began thinking about friends who leave and go overseas. I began to wonder what someone would do if her best friend left to go overseas without saying goodbye. How worried would that person be? How far would she go to make sure her friend was ok?

Glynne MacLean

To Mum

1. WHERE IS ASHA?

Where is Asha? Katina wondered. Why hasn't she come to afternoon classes? She never got sick. Her parents were strict about her coming to school, so she wouldn't still be working at her morning job cleaning tortoise shells and mending fish traps. Where was she then? It felt strange without Asha sitting next to her.

"Katina Alexis!" The teacher's bark made Katina drop her reed pen. She gulped and said, "Yes, miss?"

The teacher's black eyes burned like coals. Her top lip curled upward as she began to speak. "Stop daydreaming, Katina, and answer the question."

Katina's voice was as quiet as she could make it and still be heard. "Would you repeat the question, please?"

The teacher's nostrils flared. "Name the three most important spices that come through our port from India on their way to the Byzantine Empire and Arabia?"

Katina exhaled with relief. That was easy. Even without paying attention to the lesson, Katina knew the answer to that. Asha's father, Mr. Patel, was a spice trader at the port. "Pepper, cinnamon, and cloves, miss."

The teacher snorted, as if disappointed that Katina knew the answer. "Very well," she said, turning back to the rest of the class. "That will do for today. Tomorrow you'll need to bring an abacus. Don't forget."

Katina retrieved her pen from the cool tile floor. She put it and her scroll into her satchel and followed the other girls out into the narrow, shady streets of Suq, still worrying about Asha. The warm air was filled with the calls of street sellers and donkey drivers. "Clear the way. Coming through," they shouted.

Outside the three-story building that housed the boys' classes, Katina leaned on the warm, mudbrick wall and waited. She wanted to ask Asha's older brother, Sachin, if Asha was ok.

The sea breeze curled between the tall buildings, carrying the smells of the town. Katina picked out the sharp aroma of seaweed from last night's storm, marshy river mud, and smoke from cooking fires. She also caught a sweet whiff of cinnamon, the sharpness of pepper, and the rich tang of donkey droppings. Katina loved the complex smells of Suq, her hometown. It made her feel as if the whole world was passing through her island home.

She was up on her tiptoes now, trying to spot Sachin as the boys belted out of their classroom, joking and laughing. He wasn't among them. Hadn't he gone to school either? Had something happened at Asha's home? Had there been an accident? Worse still, had someone died? There was nothing else to do but to go to the Patels' house and find out.

Katina ran through the streets, dodging chickens, beggars, donkey dung, street sellers, and groups of women shopping for the evening meal. Following the salty smell of the sea, she made her way through the narrow, winding streets down to the port. An array of sea-going boats was moored there: teak baglas from India, Roman corbitas from Byzantium, and Arabian markabs. Each boat was a hive of activity as workers unloaded spices and wood from the Indian boats onto the dock. From there they loaded the goods onto the waiting Arabian and Egyptian boats to be shipped north.

Most days, Katina would have stopped to drink in the sight of exotic goods from distant lands far across the sea. She liked to watch the traders bargain over their cargoes. She'd try to guess which trader was winning as their voices began to spiral excitedly, like smoke rising from a new-born fire. Most days, she would trail her hand across the shiny coolness of the tortoise shells for sale as she passed them by, but not today.

Today she skirted around the back of the port to the edge of the town's Indian quarter, past the brightly colored Hindu temple covered with carvings of Indian gods staring out through painted eyes. There were so many carvings crowded together that Katina often wondered how they didn't push each other off. They were so different from the single carved cross outside her family's church, but today she didn't give them a thought.

The food sold in the Indian quarter usually made Katina's stomach rumble, and she would dawdle past the stalls selling flaky bread that melted on your tongue. Today she barely noticed the mouth-watering smell of fish curry and tandoori chicken. All she could think of was getting to Asha's house.

The Patels' house was in one of the poorest neighborhoods of the Indian quarter. Here the mudbrick walls of the houses were worn and crumbled, long overdue for repair. The streets were speckled with broken pieces of mudbrick, and scrawny chickens pecked and scratched among them, lifting clouds of dust like tiny sandstorms.

Katina stopped outside the Patels' door. Bending forward, she rested her hands on her thighs for a moment to catch her breath. When she was no longer puffing, she straightened up and knocked on the door. Mrs. Patel answered, wearing a yellow sari edged with blue as bright as the sky. Unlike Katina's mother, who wore Roman clothes, Mrs. Patel always wore a sari. Like Katina, Asha wore a tunic and sandals. Her older sisters, the married ones, wore saris like their mother.

Mrs. Patel didn't smile or say hello. She sniffed and swallowed the way Katina did when she was trying to pretend she hadn't been crying.

"Is Asha home, please?" Katina asked.

Mrs. Patel sniffed again and then shook her head.

"When will she be back, please?"

Mrs. Patel fluttered her long hands in front of her face, like the beating wings of a bird. She didn't speak. When Katina opened her mouth to ask again, Mrs. Patel shook her head, turned away, and gently shut the door. Katina stared at the worn wood for a while, trying to put her jumbled thoughts in order.

Asha had told her that Mrs. Patel liked her. Mrs. Patel thought Katina was a good influence. Usually, she invited Katina in and gave her gooey sweets and crunchy nibbles to eat. Something bad must have happened. Perhaps Mrs. Patel thought Katina had done something bad?

But what?

Anyway, that didn't explain why Asha wasn't at school or at home. Katina wriggled her toes in her sandals as she tried to think.

Where was Asha? Could she be at home but not allowed to see Katina?

Katina took two steps back to look up at the house and called out as loudly as she could, "Asha! Are you there? It's Katina! Asha?"

The only answers were a squawk from a startled chicken and the distant cry of seagulls.

Katina tried again. No face appeared at any of the narrow windows. There was no answering call from Asha. Not even a whisper on the breeze.

Again Katina called, but this time it was Sachin's name she used. Again, no answer. She kept yelling until a neighbor's door opened and a grizzled old woman in a faded green sari appeared, shaking a broom at her and screeching something in a language Katina didn't understand. She thought of asking about Asha, but the woman advanced on her, waving the broom like a sword.

Katina raised her hands and murmured an apology as she backed down the street a few paces. Still the old woman screeched at her, baring front teeth broken into points like fangs. She hurled her broom, and Katina ducked, turned, and took off back the way she'd come.

Though her heart was pounding like a drum, Katina didn't stop running until she got back to the port. Then she slowed to a walk, wondering what to do next.

Around her, the port workers were finishing up for the day. They no longer swarmed on and off the boats, bent under huge loads balanced on their backs. Now they stood in groups, talking and nodding, wiping their brows before heading off in ones and twos.

Katina glanced at the sun. It was lower than she'd realized. The departing workers cast tall shadows like skinny giants that followed them home. She was late. Katina was supposed to help with dinner. Her mother would be starting to worry or, worse still, starting to get angry. She was always telling Katina how hard her father and brothers worked, out fishing all day. She always said that a good dinner on the table was the least she and Katina could do for the family providers.

Katina hurried home, hoping that her mother wouldn't be angry. Maybe, she thought, just maybe, her mother would know where Asha was.

2. A CLUE

Asha wasn't at Katina's when she got home, and her mother hadn't seen her either. That night, lying in bed listening to the wind howl in from the sea, Katina tried to make sense of what had happened at the Patels'. Had Mrs. Patel been crying? Was it that she didn't want Asha to see Katina? None of it made sense. No matter which way Katina looked at it, it didn't add up. There must be something missing. Trying to work it out made Katina feel as if she were fumbling around in the dark, looking for an oil lamp to light her way.

Perhaps she was worrying too much? Katina crossed her fingers, rolled onto her side, and tucked her fingers under her pillow. Surely, she told herself, Asha would be at school tomorrow. Everything would be all right.

Katina was just drifting off to sleep when something woke her up. For a minute, she couldn't figure out what it was. The wind had dropped to a gentle rustle, and above it, all she could hear was the murmur of her parents' voices, rising and falling in the darkness. Then she heard it again—Asha's name. Her parents were talking about Asha! As quietly as she could, Katina lifted her head off her pillow and strained to hear.

Disjointed snatches of conversation reached her. She heard her father say, ". . . a wealthy Alexandrian. A merchant . . . made his money trading dates, salt, and . . . for spices. They say he has two children, but his wife died last year."

Now her mother's voice, soft but clearly audible, "It's terrible when children lose their mother."

Her father rumbled something that sounded like agreement and then said more loudly, "He claims he wants study companions for them . . . children from poor families here who can read and write . . . take them back to Alexandria."

Katina sat bolt upright.

"It's such a long way away," her mother said, "but I suppose they can earn money to send home."

"Earn money?" Her father snorted.

Her mother's voice still carried clearly. "Well, you said he wanted the children from here to be study companions and servants for his children . . ."

"Servants, my foot!" her father interrupted. "They'll not be paid a single coin!"

"Shush. You'll wake Katina. It's Mrs. and Mr. Patel I feel sorry for. What a dreadful thing to be forced into doing. We should be thankful we can afford to feed and educate all of our children."

"They'll be slaves! You can be sure of that!" exclaimed her father.

There was a rustle of blankets, and Katina heard no more conversation. She remained as still as a stone, in case they started to talk again, but all she heard was the wind. Some time later, her father began to snore and only then did Katina lie down again. She couldn't believe it, and yet . . . and yet it made a horrible sort of sense.

Katina shivered and gathered her blankets up around her chin. Asha and Sachin were the two youngest of seven children. Though Mr. Patel had a good job as a spice trader at the port, they never had much money, especially during the summer monsoon when the port was closed.

Katina had never thought of them as poor, but then she remembered Asha talking about how much her father had paid out for dowries when Asha's older sisters got married. Asha had said her family wouldn't have enough money for her to get married, but Katina hadn't believed her.

She should have listened. Now it might be too late. Were Asha and Sachin being sent to Alexandria?

Alexandria. That was in Egypt in the Byzantine Empire! Katina had no idea how many months it would take to sail there from Socotra, but she knew that it was a very long way away. Not as far away as China, where Suq's shipwreck bell had come from, but further away than she could imagine. They wouldn't return for years and years. If ever.

No! Katina wouldn't believe it. Mrs. Patel wouldn't sell her children to be slaves. Her mother had said that the merchant had promised that the children would be servants and earn money. Sachin's oldest brother was working in Arabia. Every three months, he sent his wages back to

Socotra. If Asha's parents believed the merchant was offering their children work as well as an education, they might have agreed. No wonder Mrs. Patel was upset.

Katina didn't sleep a wink. She kept turning her parents' conversation over and over in her mind, getting more and more scared for Asha. The one thing she was certain of was that she needed a plan to find out exactly what had happened to Asha.

At first light the next morning, Katina cooked a breakfast of fried eggs and fish steaks for her father and brothers and put stage one of her plan into action.

"Papa, may I come down to the lagoon with you this morning? I can spend the morning helping Auntie weave fish traps."

"Why do you want to do that?" asked Thomas, her oldest and least favorite brother.

Katina shrugged. "For a change." She wasn't going to remind him that Asha also worked mornings on the beach.

Her father yawned and stretched. "I don't see why not. Some fresh air will do you good." He waggled a finger scarred by an accident with a filleting knife. "Mind you, you'd better make yourself useful. No twiddling your thumbs on the beach while your mother is back here collecting the water and doing the housework."

Hector, her favorite brother, held out a warm hand, leathery and rough, hardened by years of hauling in waterlogged sails and fishing nets. "Come along then, Kati. The ocean waits for no one. We've got to catch the outgoing tide, and we can't keep the boys waiting. If their bosses don't turn up for work, they take the day off quicker than the trade wind will put out an oil lamp."

Katina stood on the shore, with the wind whipping sand around her legs, and watched as Hector, Thomas, and her father launched their fishing dhows. To the west, the sky was a deep purple—so dark that a few stars still shone. To the east, the first rays of the rising sun were softening the color to a dusky gray-blue.

As soon as the dhows were afloat, each skipper began to haul up and set the boat's single sail. Katina waved goodbye as the three sails billowed, swinging the family's boats sideways to the wind.

Then she took off at a run, her cloak flying behind her like a fourth sail. By the mouth of the inlet, Katina flopped down beside her aunt, who was sorting traps to be mended. They leaned up against a driftwood log smoothed by long years of wind-blown sand and waited for the sun to rise over the horizon.

When Auntie lifted the lid on a pail of her famous fish stew, the cool morning air was filled with the smell of saffron, fish, and sweet potato. She poured it out through a cloth sieve, removing the bones and the remains of fish heads and tails, leaving a thick, sweet liquid that warmed Katina from her nose to her toes. It was delicious.

While they ate, Katina watched the birds fishing and pecking in the muddy banks of the inlet. Hector said that birds were the fishermen of the sky. He'd taught Katina how to tell a visiting white crowned osprey from a local Barbary falcon by its yellow-rimmed eyes.

Katina's favorite feathered visitors were the migrating pink flamingos that stopped off in Socotra to fuel up before taking flight again. Their raucous bickering was so loud that when they departed it felt as if the whole island went silent. A chill ran down Katina's spine as she thought of Asha and Sachin migrating or, worse still, being made into slaves.

As soon as it was light enough, Auntie gave Katina a pile of flexible branches from the white berry bushes that grew on the island and told her to strip off the leaves. When they were bare, Katina began weaving the supple branches into arrowhead-shaped fish traps. It was tedious work needing a lot of finger strength, and Katina had to take care not to snap or crack the wood.

For a while, Auntie watched her work. Then, once she was sure Katina hadn't forgotten how to weave traps, she set to work herself, fixing holes and retying weak spots in the old traps.

The moment Auntie turned her back, Katina bounced to her feet. She shaded her eyes, peering at the group of girls beginning their morning's work cleaning tortoise shells. Asha wasn't among them. Katina sat down and bent over her task once more. Glancing sideways, she saw Auntie give her a long, hard look, as if to say, you're here to work, my girl.

All morning, Katina kept an eye out for Asha, but she was nowhere to be seen. Each time one of the other women or girls came past, Katina asked them if they'd seen Asha. No one had. Most people she asked shrugged or turned away, but Katina couldn't help but notice that a few of them looked instinctively to where the dark-timbered foreign boats, with their strange square sails, were moored at the port.

3. THE CORBITA

By lunchtime Katina's fingers were aching. The skin of her knuckles was criss-crossed with little scratches and reddened with light grazes. Katina barely noticed. With each passing hour that Asha didn't appear, Katina's stomach tightened, clenching like a fist. She had to do something! The moment Auntie began to stoke the fire for lunch, Katina excused herself, saying she had to collect her abacus for school.

Instead of going home, she dashed down to the port, determined to find out if Asha was aboard the Alexandrian corbita. She threaded her way through the throngs of sweaty workmen, bent under the weight of spice sacks, and skirted the gangs hauling on the rope-operated cranes, swinging bundles of logs from deck to dock. Up close, their guttural chants of heave-ho, heave-ho were loud enough to drown out the cries of donkey drivers and haggling traders, counterpointed by the sharp note of the foreman's commands.

Katina ducked, hoping to avoid detection. Only workers were allowed on the dock. She passed the two Arabian markabs with their sewn planks and single masts and stopped opposite the last ship in the port. It was a corbita—a Roman cargo ship.

Compared with her family's fishing dhows, it was colossal, looming over her and casting a shadow that stretched right across the dock and up over the cargo warehouses. It was a heavily constructed ship of nailed dark timber with sturdy horizontal planks that wrapped around the exterior of the hull. Her father had told Katina that these planks were called wales. Their job, he'd said, was to strengthen the hull in high seas.

The steering oars on the markabs were attached to the stern, but the corbita's steering oars protruded from holes high up in the hull. At the dock, they had been hauled onboard and chained so that only the ends of the massive oars stuck out like crabs' eyes.

Katina stood on tiptoes, trying to see the deck, but it was no use. She just wasn't tall enough. She'd had no idea it would be so big. It looked massive enough to mow down anything that got in its way. Katina's throat went dry.

She took a step backward and collided with a donkey laden with amphoras. The animal brayed its outrage, stamping its feet and rattling the clay jugs, but Katina didn't give the driver a chance to tell her off. She made a dash for the stairs of the nearest warehouse. At the top, she glanced back over her shoulder. The donkey driver was shaking his fist at her, but he wasn't chasing her.

Katina maneuvered between the bolts of cotton and stacked amphoras in the open warehouse doorway until she was again opposite the corbita, but now she was able to look down on it. Wedged between two sacks of sweet-smelling cinnamon, she leaned over the railing and scanned the scrubbed deck of the ship.

It had a single mast with a horizontal, stiff-looking yard, or spar, on which to rig the sail. Roman soldiers stood at each end of the vessel, with another at the gangplank and a fourth on the roof of the galley. They were watching everything. Katina inhaled sharply. As if expecting trouble, each soldier rested a hand on the hilt of his sword. None of the other boats had guards of any kind, let alone Roman soldiers.

There was no sign of Asha, Sachin, or any other children. There was also no sign of the owner. Only dock workers and guards. Katina could see a wisp of smoke rising from the galley, but the open doorway was too deep in shadow for Katina to make out who was cooking. She had no way of telling if Asha and Sachin were below deck, and the presence of the guards meant she had no chance of getting aboard. She couldn't implement stage two of her plan.

What should she do next? Should she try and find Mr. Patel and ask him? No. Asha wasn't allowed to bother him at work, and Katina's father was the same. Work time was for working. It wasn't for standing around answering questions.

There had to be something she could do. Katina's throat closed up, and she felt tears pricking at the back of her eyes. She bit her lip and sniffed. Crying wasn't going to help. There had to be someone she could ask. Someone who would tell her the truth, rather than just what he thought she was old enough to hear.

As she searched the throng below for inspiration, someone rapped her on the shoulder, and she turned to see a burly dock worker with a ferocious scowl, shaking his jowls at her. He made a throat-slitting gesture with a filthy finger and jabbed it towards an exit between two warehouses.

Katina took off. She was halfway home when she heard someone calling her name, and she ground to a halt, almost losing her balance as her sandals slid sideways. Her friend, Unice Nepos, caught her arm just in the nick of time. For a few moments, the girls leaned against each other, giggling.

"Where's your abacus?" Unice asked. "The teacher will throw a fit if you've forgotten it."

"I was just going home to get it."

"I'll come with you. I hate going to school on my own."

As they walked, Unice waved a beautifully wrapped parcel beneath Katina's nose, filling her nostrils with the enticing aroma of cheese straws. "Lunch?" offered Unice. "I have plenty. I asked Cook to wrap an extra helping for you. We can eat as we go."

In spite of the tension in her stomach, Katina's mouth watered. Breakfast had been hours ago. She unwrapped a corner of the cotton parcel Unice handed her and extracted a still warm cheese straw. With each crunch, its crispness melted into a gooey mouthful of cheesy delight.

Before Unice arrived on the island, Katina had never heard of cheese straws. The Nepos family was one of the few on Socotra wealthy enough to import wheat flour. In fact, it took only one glance at the fine fabric of Unice's tunic and its jeweled clasps to see that she was the daughter of a rich man.

What really set the Nepos family apart from the rest of the Socotra population was their blue eyes. They were among the very few blue-eyed people the islanders had ever seen. Katina thought their fear of the Nepos' blue eyes was founded in foolish superstition, but most of the townsfolk made it a point to avoid the family.

"Yum," said Katina, licking her lips.

Unice slipped her free arm through Katina's. "Have you heard about Asha? She's so lucky. I wish it was me."

Katina stopped, a shortened straw halfway to her mouth. She searched Unice's face for any sign of sarcasm, but her expression was wistful, almost sad.

"You know about Asha?" Katina asked. "It's true then?"

Unice nodded, her mouth full.

"I don't understand," said Katina, as she started walking again. "It's terrible, not lucky."

"Terrible?" exclaimed Unice. "Hardly. I'd love to go to Alexandria. My papa says it's the second best city in the whole world." She twisted another straw free of her parcel.

"How do you know?" asked Katina. "About Asha, I mean."

"She told me," said Unice airily.

Katina frowned. *She* was Asha's best friend, not Unice. Asha told *Katina* her secrets, not Unice.

Unice had never even been to Asha's house. She wasn't a best friend. She wasn't Katina's, and she wasn't Asha's.

"When did she tell you?" Katina asked.

"Don't you believe me?" Unice had finished her own parcel of cheese straws and was now eyeing Katina's.

Katina glanced down. She still had six left. Six delicious treats that Unice had asked her cook to make especially for Katina. Katina's mother always said, if you're going to accept gifts from people, the least you can do is be nice to them. Katina didn't believe that Asha had told Unice anything that she had not already discussed with Katina. That was the problem with Unice. She was so eager to be liked that often she'd say whatever she thought Katina, Asha, or the teacher wanted to hear, rather than what she actually knew.

So how *did* Unice know that Asha was off to Alexandria? Did she know or was it a guess? Her information certainly added up with the conversation Katina had overheard between her parents.

Katina wrinkled her nose as she paused outside her house. If only she could be sure, but how?

"I didn't say I didn't believe you," she said at last. "These are wonderful, thank you. Please thank your cook for me."

"Better grab your abacus," Unice said. "I'll wait out here but hurry up. We'll have to run all the way to make it to school on time."

4. ALEXANDRIA BOUND?

By the time the girls got to school, class had already started. Katina opened the door, hoping against hope that Asha would be in her usual seat. She wasn't. Helena was sitting there, twisting a strand of her hair around and around her finger.

Katina felt the back of her neck prickle as a pair of eyes bored into her spine, and she turned slowly to see the teacher tapping her foot. As Katina opened her mouth to apologize, the teacher raised a hand to silence her.

The teacher let the silence expand before asking, in a dangerously quiet voice, "Katina Alexis and Unice Nepos. Where have you been?"

"Looking for Asha, miss," Katina answered.

The teacher snorted, but Katina hurried on with her explanation, her words tumbling one over another like monsoon rain off a roof. "She's gone. I've looked everywhere. She's gone—"

"Yes," snapped the teacher. "She has gone. I'm well aware of that. If you two had bothered to arrive on time, you would have heard my announcement. I suppose now I will have to waste everybody's time and repeat it. Asha Patel has left. She has left Socotra."

Left Socotra. So it was true. Asha and Sachin were bound for Alexandria. The horrible truth wrapped itself around Katina, squeezing her chest and throat so that she could hardly breathe.

Unice nudged her. "I told you so."

"Don't whisper in my class," bellowed the teacher. "Asha has gone to work in Alexandria. She is most fortunate. She will have access to an education in the greatest city in the world."

The teacher pointed to their desks. "Sit down," she snapped, before throwing her hands in the air. "What on earth are you crying about, Katina Alexis?"

All Katina could manage between sniffs was, "Asha gets seasick. She—"

"Asha will be fine," interrupted the teacher. "Stop making such a fuss. We live on a small island. People come and go. You just have to get used to it. Asha has her older brother with her, and I'm sure he'll take car of her. Now dry your eyes and sit down, the both of you. Enough, I say."

All afternoon, Katina's thoughts kept returning to the fact that Asha had gone. She would never see her again, and she hadn't even said goodbye.

The lesson was over and their abacuses stowed under their desks before Katina realized that the teacher had said Asha was going to *work* in Alexandria. She hadn't said Asha and Sachin were going to be slaves. Katina replayed her parents' conversation in her mind. Her mother had said they were to be servants. It was only her father who'd thought they were going to be slaves.

Who was right?

Was the teacher only saying what she thought the students were old enough to hear? She had often said that sugar-coating the truth was pointless. In the teacher's opinion, the sooner children learned about the realities of life, the better equipped they'd be to cope. Did that mean that it was Katina's father who had gotten his lines crossed in the wind?

Katina heaved a sigh. If she could be sure that Asha was leaving for a better life, full of excitement and opportunities, her departure would be bearable. However, if she was destined for a miserable future as a slave, Katina would have to find a way to rescue her.

First, Katina had to discover the truth.

How would she do it?

On their way home to Unice's house, Unice put a comforting arm around her shoulders. "I know you'll miss Asha, but it won't be so terrible. I can be your new best friend. It'll be ok, I promise. Just think, you can come over to my house, and I can visit yours. It would be better if you come to mine, though. We can dress up in Mama's clothes and try on her jewelry. Papa says he'll buy you a laughing dove just like mine. We'll keep them together at my house. Together forever—just like us."

When Katina didn't answer, Unice's lower lip began to tremble. "Don't you want to be my friend, Katina?" she asked, her voice quivering like a blossom in the wind.

"I do," murmured Katina. "It's just . . . Asha and Sachin . . ." she trailed off, not wanting to say it aloud, in case doing so would somehow make it true.

"Are you angry because she didn't say goodbye to you?" Unice asked.

"I'm not angry—" began Katina.

"She didn't say goodbye to me either," Unice interrupted. "Not really. I just heard my parents talking. I didn't think you'd believe me, so I said she'd told me. I didn't think that would hurt you. I just . . ." Unice sniffed and wiped her eyes.

"Don't cry," Katina said. "I'm not angry, not with you or Asha. I'm just really, really worried. Yes, I do wish that Asha had said goodbye. Her mother was crying when I went to her house yesterday after school, and then last night, my papa said they were going to be slaves. Asha and Sachin—slaves. It's terrible."

"They're not going to be slaves," said Unice, shaking her head emphatically. "Slaves can't read and write. I should know. None of our slaves can read or write. My papa says it's a waste of time for them to learn things they're never going to use."

"You don't have slaves," protested Katina. "Do you?"

Unice rolled her red-rimmed eyes. "Cook's a slave. So are the houseboys. We've always had slaves."

Katina ran a hand through her thick shoulder-length hair. It didn't make sense. She'd seen slaves at the port. They'd all worn a sense of hopelessness like a uniform. Katina wasn't sure if it was their shuffling gait, the droop of their heads, or their downcast eyes, but there'd been a depressing sameness about them.

Unice's cook wasn't anything like that. She was always cheerful and lively, always smiling, and her laugh was so infectious that everyone within earshot caught it. As for the Nepos' houseboys, in the absence of adults, they were like any other boys her age—rowdy, irritating, and boastful.

"Your cook's a slave?" Katina asked. "Are you sure?"

"Yes! Of course I'm sure. Cook's our responsibility. Well, my papa's responsibility. He owns her, so he has to take care of her—food, clothing, a place to live, all of that. I told you she can't read or write. Slaves don't. Asha and Sachin can."

Katina wished she felt as confident as Unice. For a moment she considered asking her father what he thought, but she soon dismissed the idea. She couldn't admit she'd been listening in on his conversation.

There had to be someone who knew. Someone who'd had dealings with the Alexandrian merchant. Someone at the port maybe. Then Katina had a brainwave. She'd ask the dock manager, Mr. Dumas. If she dropped Unice off at her house and didn't stay to play, she'd have time to go by the port on her way home.

Katina climbed the steps from the street up to the first-floor balcony of the port warehouses. She couldn't help but glance across at the corbita lit by the late afternoon sun. The soldiers were still in place and still alert, watching everything and everyone, even though loading was finished for the day. The dock below was crowded, but bargaining and general day's-end chatter had replaced the sounds of heavy lifting.

A waft of fresh pepper tickled at Katina's nose, and she sneezed her way past an open storeroom housing a massive mound of pepper to scan the throng for Mr. Dumas. His shock of white hair and long neck always made him easy to spot. He was as conspicuous as a great white egret in a flock of brown-necked ravens, but today there was no sign of him.

Katina moved on past bolts of cotton, barrels of ghee, and a myriad of spices to the end of the building. It was no use. No matter which way she looked, Mr. Dumas was nowhere to be seen.

As the workmen and traders began to disperse for home, Katina made her way back along the balcony to the corbita. The gangplank had been raised for the night, and a mountain of cargo remained on the dock, covered in sacking anchored by a rope lattice weighted down with large stones. The soldiers, ever watchful, stood guard on the deserted deck. For the first time all day, the tightness in Katina's stomach loosened a little.

Cargo boats left Socotra when they were full—so full that the crew had to sleep on deck—and not before. This vessel's gangplank was up, which meant that the crew members were aboard but obviously below deck, and there was still cargo to be loaded.

Katina smiled. Time was on her side. She had time to discover the truth.

5. INFORMATION GATHERING

When Katina woke up the next morning, the wind was whistling through the narrow streets like an old man's breath through his broken front teeth. Katina liked the wind. She loved the way it whipped up the waves, shook the date palms, and chased sand up and down the streets of Suq. To Katina, the wind was power. The wind was freedom.

Most of the residents of Socotra, however, dreaded the wild wind that blew non-stop, day and night, during the summer monsoon. For three months, it howled off the mountains, hurling itself across the island many times faster than the fastest camels could gallop. It herded up the sand with ferocity and threw it in the islanders' faces. It tortured the sea and tormented the animals.

Today it was only strong enough to make small objects tumble and raise white caps on the sea. Katina wasted no time in worrying over the havoc it might wreak on her hair. She could wear it loose and let it fly free.

An hour after sunrise, she set off with her mother for the market. The wind was twisting the cries of the stallholders, flapping their tunics and rattling their wares in the already bustling market. While her mother haggled over the price of figs, Katina went to collect the cloth her mother had ordered to sew tunics for the family.

She already had the precious cloth under her arm when a thought struck her and she glanced around the busy street. A pair of donkey drivers were discussing the weather. A tall woman examined the base of a metal cooking pot, closely watched by the wizened salesman, as her three children played peekaboo behind her stola. A group of sari-clad ladies compared bracelets, and two small boys were chasing an excited chicken around and around a reeking cheese stand. The only eyes on Katina were those of a superior-looking cat perched in the slit of an upper-story window.

Katina ducked down a side street, telling herself that a detour by the port wouldn't take long. No one would miss her.

Katina stood on tiptoes and peered through the gates of the port. Just like yesterday, the dock was a hive of noise and activity. The corbita was docked third in line and hidden behind two Arabian markabs, the nearest of which was being readied for departure. On the opposite bank, Katina could see the team of bulls that would pull the boat into the center of the inlet. Unlike the port workers, the bulls seemed half asleep. They stood motionless, the only sign of life the occasional flick of a tail to scatter the hovering flies.

Katina looked left, then right, and spotted Mr. Dumas, bobbing his head vigorously as he issued instructions to a foreman. Katina giggled. Asha was right. He really did look like a great white egret. Mr. Dumas swapped cargo leftovers with her father for fish, and whenever Katina was sent to deliver the fish, she struggled to keep a straight face as he bobbed and nodded, continually stepping from one foot to the other.

Mr. Dumas finished his conversation and turned toward the gate. Katina waved, bouncing up and down, and he waved back, grinning broadly.

"Katina Alexis?" he called. "Is that you? Are you off to the market?"

"Yes, Mr. Dumas. I've picked up cloth for Mama."

Mr Dumas shook his head, cupping a hand around his ear to indicate he couldn't hear her. "Stay there. I'll come over."

"I'm glad I caught you," he began when he reached her. "Would you be so kind as to ask your papa if he can spare me three or four of those fabulous jack fish he's so famous for? I have a few merchants coming over for dinner tonight. One is an important man with business interests across all of the Byzantine Empire and beyond." He waggled a finger at Katina. "There's nothing quite like good food to oil a bargain or two."

Katina nodded, wondering if the important man might be the Alexandrian. She was about to ask, but she quickly changed her mind. It wouldn't help to look nosy. Instead, she asked, as casually as she could, when the corbita was leaving.

"If everything goes as planned, we'll have it loaded within the next three days," said Mr. Dumas, scratching under his chin. "It takes a lot of cargo to fill one of those. Mind you, the captain tells me its cargo capacity is tiny compared to the corbitas that ply the Mediterranean. They must be a sight to see."

"Do you know if there are any children aboard, Mr. Dumas?" asked Katina, twisting her hands together anxiously.

"Two or three, I think. Off to Alexandria. Bit of an adventure, wouldn't you say?" he asked, raking a hand through his thick white hair so that it stood up on end, just like the raised crest of an egret.

Katina swallowed the giggle that threatened to bubble out of her mouth. She needed more information, and Mr. Dumas might just be the person in the know. "What do you think they'll be doing? The children, I mean."

"Depends, I suppose. I saw a young Indian lad at the top of the corbita's gangplank this morning. He looked very businesslike. He was writing down everything that was being loaded and where it was being stowed. I'd say he was working as a scribe, wouldn't you?"

Katina was about to ask if the young man was Sachin when someone bellowed for Mr. Dumas.

"Got to go," said Mr. Dumas, bobbing cheerily as he turned to go. "Bring one of your brothers with you when you drop off the fish this evening. I have a sack of rice for your mama."

Katina wound her way back to the market, mulling over Mr. Dumas's words. Had he seen Sachin working as a scribe? Sachin paid attention to detail. He liked noting down facts and figures, and Asha often boasted that he had the neatest writing in his class. He'd make a good scribe. Was that why the Alexandrian merchant had chosen him? If it were, did that mean he wasn't a slave? Katina had never heard of a scribe being a slave.

As she rounded the next corner, Katina saw her mother talking to an elegant woman with stylish braided hair. Though her back was turned to Katina, it was obvious from the way the other morning shoppers had retreated around them that the elegant woman was Mrs. Nepos. In the midst of the bustling market, the two women stood isolated, as if in a sun-drenched clearing in a dense jungle. No one brushed past them. No one asked them to step aside. No one came within arm's length of them.

As Katina drew closer, she heard murmurings of prayers in Greek and Sanskrit to ward off the evil eye. A number of people were fingering protective charms. Young and old watched Mrs. Nepos while pretending to go about their business.

"Ah, there you are," called Katina's mother as she saw her. She held out a hand and drew Katina into their charmed circle.

"Hello, Mrs. Nepos," Katina said.

Mrs. Nepos smiled, lightening the sternness of her face for a moment. Her fine nose, thin lips, and elaborately braided hair reminded Katina of the nobles she'd seen on Roman coins.

"Mrs. Nepos has made a very generous offer, Katina," her mother said. "Since there's no school this afternoon, she has arranged for you and Unice to visit the dragon's blood tappers."

For a second, Katina couldn't believe her ears. She looked from her mother to Mrs. Nepos and back again, and then all of her questions came tumbling out.

"Into the wilds? Really? Are we going on camel-back? Will it be dangerous? Who else is going?" For as long as she could remember, Katina had longed to see beyond the protective town walls. She knew that on either side of the island's mountain backbone there were caves, desert, and open land where cattle grazed. She'd seen glimpses of them from the sea when out fishing with her brothers, but she had never set foot outside the walls of Suq.

The two mothers laughed and told her she would soon have her answers. Then they bid each other goodbye. Katina was instructed to go home, collect her lightweight cotton cloak and goatskin water carrier, and meet Unice at the town gates. Her mother warned her not to take chances with the sun and to wear her cloak with the hood up while out in the open. Katina promised she would.

When Katina passed on the message about the fish for Mr. Dumas, her mother assured her she would be back in time to deliver the fish with Hector. Then she shooed Katina off with a final reminder to behave herself and remember to say thank you.

6. INTO THE WILDS

Katina arrived at the open town gates breathless with excitement. From their shelter, she could see the stony land give way to hazy desert rippled into dunes by the relentless wind. Beyond that rose the craggy mountains, their tops hidden by fast-moving clouds. On their lower slopes, in the partially shaded gullies, the famous dragon's blood trees grew. That was their destination this morning. Katina could hardly believe it.

She glanced up at the guards. They were bent over a board game, their backs turned to the wilds. For a moment, Katina wondered what they were supposed to be guarding against. People coming into Suq? People leaving? Either way, they didn't seem to think any threat was worth caring about today.

Katina took a deep breath and, for the first time in her life, stepped through the gates of her hometown. To her left, a camel snorted, and she whirled to face it as a trill of laughter sounded from the same direction.

"Don't be scared." Unice was calling out from the back of the second of three camels. She looked as exotic as a foreign princess, the reins held casually loose in her hands. Her saddlecloth was woven in bright colors and edged with long golden tassels that danced with each movement the camel made. As if not wanting to be outdone, the threads of silk in Unice's cloak glittered like tiny jewels as they caught the sun. Two large bundles were strapped on either side of the camel, behind the raised wooden saddle back.

Unice's older brother, Nate, stood holding the bridles of the other two camels. One crouched on the ground, its legs folded beneath it, as Unice's family cook fussed over the contents of its packs. The last camel, the palest of the three, was burdened only by a saddle. It held its head high, its dark eyes half-hidden beneath the longest lashes Katina had ever seen.

Now Katina became aware that Nate's bright blue eyes were glaring at her, as if to make it clear that it wasn't his idea to have his little sister and her friend tag along. Nate was ten years older than Unice and the only one of her brothers to have come with the family to Socotra. The others were working in Alexandria, Byzantium, and as far away as Rome.

"Isn't this wonderful?" Unice asked from on high. Katina glanced back at Nate. He was waving his finger at the camel packs as if mentally checking off their contents. When he lifted his arm, she could see the hilt of a short sword strapped to his belt. Katina was used to fishermen carrying knives, but she'd never been so close to anyone wearing a weapon. For a moment she hesitated, and then she remembered what Unice once said about him. Nate's sharp features might make him look as fierce as a wasp, she had said, but he didn't sting.

"Don't tell me you're dumbstruck, Katina Alexis," said Unice with a giggle.

"Sort of," Katina admitted. "I've never been out here. Have you?"

Cook appeared from behind the seated camel. Where Nate's and Unice's brilliant blue eyes resembled a clear spring sky, Cook's eyes were as soft as the sea on a misty gray morning. Her tunic and cloak were undecorated and her clasps plain, but Katina noticed that the quality of the cloth was as good as what she herself wore every day.

Cook caught Katina's excited grin and smiled back at her.

"Ever ridden a camel?" Unice asked.

Katina shook her head, and her grin turned to a frown. Before any doubts could take a firm shape, Cook patted her arm with a hand calloused from years of scrubbing and stirring. "Don't worry, you're with me," she said. "We're skinny enough to both fit in the saddle, and I'll make sure you don't fall off. I've packed a delicious picnic so, if you're feeling afraid, just think about lunch."

Nate rolled his eyes. "Food—Cook's answer to everything."

Cook signaled to Katina to mount, and Katina grasped the smooth wood of the arching saddle front. Immediately, the camel twisted its head, rolling back its lips to expose yellowed teeth.

It snorted, and a cloud of spit-laden bad breath caught Katina full in the face.

"Show no fear," said Nate quietly from behind her. "If they smell that you're frightened, they'll never do as they're told. You have to be bossy without being mean. Firm but kind."

Katina wiped her face and, determined to be fearless, clambered onto the crouching animal. Nate showed her where to hold on while Cook eased herself in between Katina and the curve of the saddle back. She put an arm around Katina's waist and flipped the reins over Katina's head as Nate flicked the camel's haunches.

The camel snorted once more, and then, grunting and grumbling, it staggered to its feet. Katina hung on tight as they careered, first right, and then left, pitching more violently than a dhow on a stormy sea. She shut her eyes and thought about the melting magic of cheese straws until at last the camel was fully upright and more or less stationary.

"You can open your eyes now."

Katina's eyes flew open to see that Unice had wheeled her camel in beside them and was chuckling in her ear. Nate's camel was now down on its knees, and with the ease of an expert, he mounted the saddle, barely tilting as his camel regained its footing.

"Thanks for asking me," said Katina as she looked around. "It's an amazing view from up here. I had no idea we'd be this high up."

"Great isn't it?" said Unice.

"No galloping, Unice," barked Nate. "I mean it," he added as she made a face. "I'll have Cook take the pair of you back if you do. I've got work to do. This is a business trip. So no mischief! Unice, fall in behind me. Cook, bring up the rear."

Cook twitched the reins, and behind her, Katina could feel one of Cook's heels nudge the bristly flank of the camel. They set off in single file, rocking gently with each step. The swaying was less violent than when the camel had first stood up, and it didn't take long for Katina to find her balance. She adjusted her center of gravity the way she did at sea in a rolling swell. When the camel rocked left, she counterbalanced to the right.

Soon she was drinking in the wild scenery as the hot wind blew sand through her hair. Beneath the cotton scarf Cook had given her to shield her nose and mouth, Katina's nostrils filled with the scents of the baking earth, so different from the spicy, smoky aromas of Suq.

A snake zipped sideways across the sand. Spiky aloe plants of all sizes dotted the landscape, and buzzards circled above, crying like old women at a funeral. All the while, the sun and the temperature rose until the clouds were all burned off the tops of the mountains. By the time Suq had vanished from view, the air was almost too hot to breathe.

Soon they could see patches of shade in the folds of the mountain's lower slopes and groves of dragon's blood trees. Unlike other trees on the island, these had no lower branches. The trunk was uninterrupted, like that of a palm tree, but, while palm fronds tilted toward the Earth, the branches of the dragon's blood tree reached for the sky, forming what looked like a dense, circular mass of roots in mid-air. It was as if they were upside down. They were definitely the oddest plant Katina had ever seen.

Four men met them in a shady grove. They shook hands with Nate, unloaded the packs from Unice's camel, and pitched two low, Bedouin-style tents. The soil in each tent was covered with vivid rugs. Then the men joined Nate in one while Unice, Katina, and Cook gathered in the other.

After a magnificent lunch, Katina and Unice lay back on the soft rugs and talked, comparing notes on what they'd seen. Cook cleared away lunch and then began grinding droplets of dragon's blood resin. The men had collected it by making little cuts in the trees' bark—the resin oozed out and then dried hard when exposed to the air.

Katina couldn't remember the last time she'd had such a lazy day. By the time Nate called them out from the tent, the sun was well past its peak. When they retraced their steps, rocking comfortably from side to side, the light had changed, and so had the landscape. Colors had softened, and shadows lingered where before it would have been too hot to stand.

On her way back, Katina saw so much more than she'd seen on the way out. She noticed the swirling movement of the sand, like the slowest of waves. She spotted darting creatures burrowing for cover as the camels approached. In the aloes, she noted flocks of tiny birds flitting through the blooms, drinking nectar.

Every now and again, she looked skyward. Behind them, the clouds were again gathering along the mountain tops, as if providing down pillows for the peaks to rest on overnight. Soaring eagles rode the thermal air currents, spiraling upward with barely a beat of their wings, as majestic as the mightiest Roman emperor.

Katina was astounded to find that a landscape she'd thought barren and empty was so full of life.

7. FAIR-WEATHER FRIENDS

It wasn't until Katina saw the walls of Suq shimmering in the distance that she realized she had not thought of Asha since leaving the port hours ago. She'd been too busy enjoying herself. Too busy drinking in the exotic wilderness, too busy lying in a tent chatting, too busy eating. All the while Asha had been doing who knows what?

What sort of friend did that make Katina? Asha had only been gone a few days, and already she'd forgotten her best friend. Would Asha forget Katina so quickly? No, Asha wouldn't do that. Asha believed in friendship forever.

When they argued, it was always Katina who would say that she didn't want to be friends anymore. Asha would disagree. She'd say that, even when your friends make mistakes, you should stand by them. That didn't mean you always had to agree with your friends, or even like what they did, but you didn't stop being friends with them.

Today Katina had barely given Asha a thought. Did that make Katina a fair-weather friend?

As the smell of spice and the salt of the sea breeze once more tickled her nostrils, Katina had a thought. She could ask Cook what it was like being a slave. She didn't know her name. She'd never heard her called anything other than Cook. If Asha became a slave, would her name disappear, too?

"If you don't mind my asking, Cook, do you have a name? I mean, like I'm Katina and Unice is Unice."

Cook laughed. "Of course I have a name. It's Leia. You can call me Leia any time you like."

"Do you mind being a slave, Leia?"

"No, I'm very fortunate. If I weren't a slave, I wouldn't have a home, food to eat, a warm bed at night, or clothes to wear. My parents were slaves, so I couldn't be anything else."

"Isn't it horrible, though, having to do as you're told all the time?" Katina asked.

"Most people have to do as they are told most of the time," Leia said. "Very few people are wealthy enough to do what they like or give orders all day. You have to do as your parents say and as your teacher says. It's a fact of life."

"You're different from the other slaves I've seen. I thought you were a servant."

Katina could feel Leia nodding behind her. "Yes, I am most fortunate. As are my family, who work for the Nepos family in Rome. In this day and age, it all comes down to who owns you. Mr. Nepos is a good and thoughtful man, so I have a good life, as does everyone who works for him. Many slaves have a terrible life. No rest, little food, and very harsh treatment. It all depends. My siblings and I are most fortunate."

"Wouldn't you rather get paid for your work?"

"I *am* paid," said Leia. "Not in coin, but in food, shelter, and clothing. It's no different from your father swapping fish for rice and ghee from the port. I swap the work I do—cooking and cleaning—for a home."

"It all comes down to who owns you then?" Katina asked.

"Exactly," Leia agreed.

Katina pondered Leia's words for awhile as she watched the walls of Suq draw nearer and nearer. They had already stopped wavering in the heat haze.

"Do you know anything about the Alexandrian merchant in port?" Katina asked.

"Ah, the lord of the corbita," said Leia, leaning closer behind her as if about to share a secret. Katina wasn't disappointed.

"I hear," said Leia, "that he's a very important man. They say that he has met the Emperor Justinian himself. It was in Byzantium. He was called in to advise on the sea routes of the spice trade, or so they say."

"The Roman Emperor?" marveled Katina. "He's met the Emperor in person? True?"

"That's what they are saying in the market."

"Wow," Katina breathed. "Do you know if the Alexandrian is a good man?"

"That I couldn't say," Leia replied. "What I can say is that, when a rich and powerful man is cruel, you always hear about it. I've not heard any such thing about the lord of the corbita."

"Have you heard if he's a good man?" asked Katina again.

"That's the problem with people," replied Leia. "They're so quick to say bad things that they forget to say good things. That's why I always tell anyone who will listen that Mr. Nepos is a good and thoughtful man."

Katina was still considering Leia's views when they dismounted by the gates of Suq. Unice threw her arms around her, telling her that now they really were best friends. She didn't seem to notice that Katina didn't say anything in reply, except thank you.

As Katina ambled down to the seafront to meet Hector, she wondered how to find out if the Alexandrian merchant was a good man.

The leading boats of the fishing fleet were already navigating the tricky break into the lagoon when she reached the beach. She shaded her eyes to scan the horizon for her brothers' sails. They weren't far off. Out by the break, she could see and hear the thunderous surf booming and roaring, as if angry to be kept from the calm lagoon.

Katina dropped down into the shade cast by a large boulder. A sea of fish was laid out nearby to dry in the sun on salt-coated clay tiles. Little kids, too young to go to school, danced around, brandishing palm fronds like miniature warriors. Their opponents were flies and a horde of seagulls eager to steal the fish. The kids charged, scattering the seagulls in a cloud of squawking, flapping outrage, and then retreated, ready to charge the moment the thieving birds swooped again. Katina couldn't tell who was making the most noise—the kids or the seagulls.

Soon a line of fishing dhows was hauled up on the beach just beyond the salt-fish battlefield. Katina joined the swarm of fishermen and their families in the heavy work of unloading the second catch of the day.

She was bent over, ferrying a pail of fish from a dhow to the holding baskets, when four brilliant blue fishy tails appeared, dangling before her eyes. The speckled silver scales of the large jack fish glittered in the sun as they swung to and fro.

Their back fins were as blue as their tails, and their yellow eyes stared, unseeing.

It was Hector with the fish for Mr. Dumas. "We can finish up here," he said. "You take these down to the port, Kati."

"Mr. Dumas has a sack of rice for Mama," said Katina, putting down her pail and stretching her cramped muscles by reaching for the sky.

Hector glanced over his shoulder and grinned. "In that case, Papa and Thomas can finish up here."

On their way to the port, Katina told Hector about her fears for Asha and Sachin. His kind face wrinkled into a frown when she said she'd heard Papa say they'd be slaves. When she asked him to find out if Mr. Dumas's dinner guest that night was the Alexandrian merchant, Hector's frown deepened even further. He didn't agree to ask Mr. Dumas, but he didn't say he wouldn't either.

At the dock, Hector collected the sack of rice while Katina watched the corbita's gangplank being raised. The soldiers looked as alert as ever, and there was no sign of Asha.

Suddenly, Katina was distracted by a torrent of angry insults. A donkey driver had a skinny trader by the scruff of his tunic and was waving him around like a dead fish. The trader's feet flailed in the air, kicking viciously, but missing his foe. A hefty workman with a huge roll of rope coiled over one shoulder intervened, and the bellowing trader was put back down on the ground. At that moment, a movement on the corbita caught the corner of Katina's eye.

She whirled around and caught a glimpse of someone of about Sachin's height ducking into the galley. "Sachin is that you?" she shouted. "Sachin are you there?"

It was no use. Her cries were drowned out by the quarrel on the dock. Katina stared at the galley doorway, willing the person to reappear. She was still staring in vain when Hector returned with Mr. Dumas in tow.

Mr. Dumas's white hair stood up on end, looking even more startled than usual. He gave Katina a jug of ghee with a cracked lip, instructing her to keep it upright so it wouldn't leak, and then he pressed a small bundle of fragrant cardamom pods, wrapped in a square of cotton, into her palm. "For your mama," he said with an egret-like bob of his head.

Katina smiled and said thank you, her eyes still on the galley.

Mr. Dumas smiled. "Here's hoping the lord of the corbita likes your papa's jack fish as much as I do," he said, moving restlessly from one foot to the other. "Please give him my thanks."

8. VIP GUESTS

The next morning, Katina was sitting on a rock-hard pew toward the front of the church, jammed in between her mother and Hector, when the low buzz of pre-service chatter died down and silence fell. Katina glanced up, expecting to see the priest making his way down the aisle, but he didn't appear. All around them, heads were turning toward the back of the church. Katina started to twist around when her mother hissed in her ear, "Sit still. Face the front."

Katina rolled her eyes, but she did as she was told. Behind her, she could hear murmurings of awe and whispered exclamations about jewelry, soldiers, weapons, and finery. A man coughed and then said loudly, in a resounding bass voice, "We are honored, honored indeed. On behalf of the citizens of Suq, welcome to our humble place of worship."

Katina was dying to turn around, but her mother had her eye focused sideways on Katina, as intent as a falcon watching its prey. Katina heaved a sigh. It wasn't as if the service had started or anything. Surely it wouldn't be disrespectful to take a quick peek. The only person who had soldiers in Suq was the lord of the corbita. Had he come to church?

Katina's concentration kept wavering all through the service. She couldn't help but wonder if the man who held Asha and Sachin's fate in his hands was just a few rows behind her. More than once her mother glared at her—a sure sign she'd been fidgeting.

Katina was determined to leap up the moment the priest passed their row as he exited, but her mother clamped a firm hand on her shoulder. By the time Katina was allowed to stand, the pews behind them were empty.

Katina scowled and then remembered she was in church and made a quick mental apology as she tried to control her disappointment. As they lined up to shake hands with the priest, Katina stood up on her tiptoes and peered all around, hoping to catch a glimpse of the lord of the corbita or his soldiers. They were nowhere to be seen. She'd missed the action. All of it!

Katina shivered as the blustery wind nipped at her arms and ankles, as if showing off the tiny teeth it had sprouted overnight. Someone tweaked at her tunic, and then Unice was dragging her out of the line waiting for the priest. "You'll never believe it," she gasped. "Never in a million years."

"The lord of the corbita was in church?" suggested Katina, her scowl returning.

Unice waved a hand. "Not *that*. Everybody knows that. This is so much better. You'll never believe it."

Katina raised her eyebrows.

"They're coming for the midday Sabbath meal!" Unice announced.

"Who?"

"The lord of the corbita and his children—"

"Children?" interrupted Katina. "His children are here? On the corbita?"

"Yes, a girl and a boy," continued Unice, her words dashing into each other in her haste. "That's what I'm trying to tell you. My papa met him last night at Mr. Dumas's dinner. Papa discovered he'd brought his children on the voyage with him. He didn't want to leave them in Alexandria so soon after their mama had died. The girl is our age, so my papa invited them for the Sabbath meal. Isn't it amazing? They say he's met the Emperor Justinian, and he's coming to our house! Can you believe it?"

Katina nodded, dumbstruck. Was that why there had been no sign of Asha? Had she been comforting a grieving girl? Did that mean Asha was ok after all?

Now another thought occurred to her. This might be her only chance to find out what kind of man the Alexandrian was. Leia had said that, when you're a slave, it all comes down to what kind of person owns you. Katina knew it wasn't polite to ask, but she just had to. For Asha's sake.

"May I come, too?" Katina asked.

Unice's mouth dropped open, and her blue eyes grew wide, like pools of bright water.

"You said I was your best friend," wheedled Katina.

Unice shut her mouth and rubbed anxiously at her nose. "I'm sorry, Katina," she said at last, "you're the wrong class. You are my best friend, I promise, but that doesn't mean you can come today. Any other day, but not today." She glanced over her shoulder. "I have to go. I've got to get changed before they arrive. Don't worry, I'll tell you all about it. Promise."

Katina stood staring after her. What did "the wrong class" mean? What was Unice talking about? She had looked really surprised, as if Katina should have known she was the wrong class. As if it were common knowledge.

The market and the port were empty as Katina walked home with her family, but the narrow streets were full of talkative people returning home after church. Her parents and brother often stopped to greet friends. The Sabbath was the only day of the week that no one worked in Suq. Even the stalls in the Hindu quarter were closed, giving everyone a day off to spend with family.

Katina stared unseeing at the road in front of her, still pondering Unice's answer. The only classes Katina had ever heard of were the classes at school. It couldn't be that because she and Unice were in the same class. What was she talking about?

It wasn't until after the midday meal that Katina plucked up enough courage to ask her mother what Unice had meant. "Don't let it worry you," said her mother, ruffling Katina's hair. "I'm sure you and Unice will still be friends. It's a special occasion, that's all."

"What did she mean, though?" insisted Katina, wrinkling her brow.

Katina's mother sighed. "She meant we're not rich. Unice's papa is the richest man in Suq. Today, he's hosting a man many times richer than he is. It's just not the kind of event that fisherfolk attend. That's all." She lifted Katina's chin with a forefinger.

"It's nothing to worry about," she said gently. "We're fisherfolk, and that's plenty good enough for us."

When Katina's frown didn't soften, her mother added, "When we've finished washing the dishes, go and get some fresh air. Take a walk along the inlet. See how many falcons you can spot. Just remember it's the Sabbath—it's not a day for running or shouting."

Katina did go for a walk, but she wasn't tempted to run or shout. She felt empty, as if she'd now lost two friends. Both her mother and Unice had said that she and Unice would still be friends, but Katina wasn't sure. Friendships weren't something to be turned on and off, depending on who is coming to visit.

She scuffed her way along the banks of the inlet, filling the toes of her sandals with damp, gritty sand, barely noticing the birds wading in the shallows or the falcons swooping and diving over the water.

Out of habit, Katina found herself walking further up the inlet toward the port. Today, the birds ruled the dock. Yesterday, it had been traders and workmen yelling and shouting, but today the birds squawked and shrieked, bickering over tidbits of discarded cargo.

The crew of the last markab in port sat dangling their legs over the side as they chatted or lazily watched the rich birdlife. As she looked up from the dockside, the markab appeared to have sprouted limbs like an octopus.

Katina climbed up to the warehouse balcony. It was easier to navigate today without cargo spilling out of open storehouses. Their doors were bolted shut, but they couldn't contain the heady scent of cinnamon, pepper, cardamom, or the rancid aroma of ghee.

The corbita came into view, and Katina spotted just two figures on guard. When she drew nearer, her heart jumped. It wasn't two soldiers on guard. It was one soldier and Sachin. The soldier stood in the stern, facing toward the town. Sachin was standing by the raised gangplank.

"Sachin?" yelled Katina, forgetting she wasn't supposed to shout today.

He made no sign he'd heard her, so she tried again, this time waving her arms around wildly, like a little kid battling seagulls.

Still Sachin didn't respond. Katina positioned herself opposite him and stared. His tunic was new. It had a narrow decorative border around the neck. He didn't look starving or browbeaten. If anything, he looked older somehow, as if he'd become an adult in just a few days. She leaned over the balcony and, cupping her hands around her mouth, bellowed with all of her might.

Sachin flinched. The soldier on the stern gave Katina a long, hard look and then returned his gaze toward the town. As Katina cupped her hands around her mouth to yell again, Sachin raised a finger to his lips. With a quick sideways nod of his head toward the soldier, he said, just loud enough for Katina to hear him, "I'm not deaf!"

"Are you ok?" asked Katina, matching his muted volume.

"I'm busy."

"Is Asha ok?"

Sachin rolled his eyes sideways in the direction of the stern and Katina turned. The soldier had unsheathed his sword. Now he raised it, reflecting the sun off the blade right into Katina's eyes. Blinded, she reeled back, her arm shielding her face.

"That's a warning," hissed Sachin. "Go—while you still can. Now!"

9. CHANCE MEETING

The soldier brandished his sword again and began to advance toward her. Katina took off down the steps and into the street. Asha would have stood her ground. She would have dared the soldier to leap from the deck onto the dock and wouldn't have budged until he'd accepted the challenge. Asha could run a lot faster than Katina, though.

Katina glanced over her shoulder. She hadn't been followed. She took a deep breath and slowed down. All around her, the streets of Suq were deserted. From open windows, Katina could hear snatches of conversation. The scent of imported Ethiopian coffee curled in and around the spicy, smoky smells of the town.

Though she enjoyed the bustle of Suq, Katina loved these few hours of daylight each week when the streets were peaceful. It made her feel as if she owned the town. She liked to make believe that she was the Empress of Suq and that after the Sabbath meal no one was allowed out until she, the Empress, said so.

Overhead, banks of baggy gray clouds were dashing away from the mountains and out to sea, as if late for an important meeting. Long, flowing tails stretched out behind them like cloaks billowing in the wind, casting fast-moving shadows across the land, as if to underline how much of a hurry they were in. One moment Katina was in a patch of sunshine, then in dappled shade, full shade, and then sunshine again.

She drifted through the streets, paying little attention to the direction in which she walked. Sachin had seemed different—older somehow. Katina's father often said there was nothing like a real job to make a boy into a man, and Katina herself had seen schoolboys join the fishing fleet and all of a sudden become too old to play with their friends left behind at school.

Katina rounded a corner and ground to a halt, unable to believe her luck. A stately procession was approaching led by a Roman soldier. Behind him was the unmistakable figure of the lord of the corbita, flanked by his children. Two more soldiers brought up the rear.

The lord wore his authority like an invisible cloak of office. Gold and jewels glinted at his throat and fingers as they caught the shifting sunlight. He was slow-marching with his shoulders back, nose tilted skyward and expression stern. His children copied his stately air, as if all too aware of their father's importance and wealth.

They, too, wore jeweled clasps and fine tunics. The girl, a skinny little thing who Katina would have thought to be younger than herself, wore a glittering headband and braids more ornate than Unice's mother's. The small boy's neck chain and round pouch gleamed as if cast in gold.

Katina waited until they drew alongside her and then darted forward. "Excuse me please," she began, but the words were barely out of her mouth when her feet left the ground. One of the soldiers bringing up the rear had picked her up by the scruff of her tunic and, without a word, dumped her out of the way. Neither the lord nor his children batted an eyelid. It was as if they'd neither seen nor heard her.

Katina bellowed after them, "I just wanted to ask you about my friend, Asha. She's my best friend, and you're taking her away. I haven't had a chance to say goodbye. I just need to know she's all right . . ."

Katina's words trailed off, dissolving into sobs. None of them had paid her the slightest bit of attention. It was as if she was just a piece of street garbage that had been swept aside—of less importance than a squashed mosquito.

She dropped to her knees, sobbing uncontrollably, and then cradled her head in her arms and wept.

A long time later, someone put her arms around her.

It was Unice. "Don't cry, Katina. Please don't cry. They're really mean. The only times they spoke to me during their whole visit was to give me orders to get them more food or clear away their plates. They're really mean and horrible. Don't mind them. It doesn't matter what they think of us. It's not important."

"I just . . . want to . . . know if A-Asha's all right," gulped Katina between sobs. "I don't care what . . . they th-think of m-me. It's A-Asha I'm wo-worried about."

"Sachin's with her," Unice said. "He'll take care of her. I know he will."

It was a long time before Unice could convince Katina to stand up. Then she put an arm around her and led her home to Leia's kitchen and sat her down by the fire.

"Oh my," said Leia, sweeping in. "Let's see if I don't have something here for drying tears. I'm sure I have just the thing."

She poured out two mugs of steaming soup, and Katina wrapped her shaky hands around her mug and took a sip. It was chicken soup, sweetened with saffron and crunchy flakes of almond. Leia didn't ask what was wrong or who'd upset her, but Katina saw her nod to Unice as if she understood exactly what the problem was.

Around sunset, Leia sent a houseboy to get Hector to come and collect Katina. Her tears were long since dried, but, though Unice and Leia had done everything they could to distract her, Katina's thoughts had stayed with Asha all afternoon.

She sifted and resifted the snippets of information she had gathered since Asha's disappearance. Though she still didn't know if Asha was going to be a slave or a servant, by the time Hector arrived, Katina had reached a decision. She had to rescue Asha. She wasn't going to be a fair-weather friend.

"You have to stop getting so worked up about things, Kati girl," said Hector as they left Unice's house. "You'll make yourself sick if you worry all the time."

"You'd help Asha and Sachin if you could, wouldn't you, Hector?" asked Katina.

Hector shrugged. "It's a done deal. A fact of life."

"I have to rescue Asha," insisted Katina. "I have to help her escape!"

Hector cleared his throat. "Aren't you forgetting the soldiers, Kati? They've been watching everything. The dock workers have been moaning about them for days. They reckon the soldiers are treating them as if they're expecting them to steal half the cargo the moment their backs are turned."

They walked in silence for a while until Katina had another thought. "What if they drop anchor overnight in the lagoon before they leave? Lots of boats do. Out in the lagoon, the soldiers won't be on guard. There's nothing to guard against."

Hector screwed up his nose as he thought, and then he shook his head. "They'll only drop anchor if they finish loading too late for the outbound tide or if it's too windy to leave. There's no guarantee it'll happen, Kati."

"If it does," persisted Katina, "will you help me rescue Asha? It'll be a full moon in a few days, and if there aren't many clouds, we can go out under the cover of darkness without any lamps."

Hector scratched his chin warily, but Katina dashed on. "We wait until the wind drops. We'll be able to judge how close we are to them by the sound of the waves against their hull. Please, Hector. It's Asha's only chance. Please. I can't ask anyone else, and I can't sail the dhow on my own, but I have to try and rescue them."

"We don't know if Asha and Sachin are going to be slaves, Kati."

"Do *you* think Papa's wrong?"

Hector made a face and then slowly shook his head. "Kati, even if we could rescue them, it's not going to solve the Patels' problem."

"It would solve Asha and Sachin's problem," Katina retorted.

"Only their immediate problem, Kati. The Patels still won't have enough income to last through the summer monsoon."

"You could employ Sachin on either side of the monsoon, couldn't you?" asked Katina. "You often say another pair of hands would make all the difference at sea. That'd help everybody."

Hector said nothing, and Katina bit her lip to stop herself from adding more. She knew not to keep on at him once he went silent like that. Like their mother, Hector took his time to absorb information before deciding on a course of action. He wasn't impulsive like Katina and her father.

Every few steps, Katina opened her mouth to speak and then remembered to keep quiet and shut it again. Hector hadn't said no, and as long as he didn't say no, there was a chance he'd help. She couldn't risk nagging.

The three-story building they shared with two other families was in sight before Hector next spoke. He took a deep sniff of the fruity smell of fig pudding wafting out into the street from their neighbor's second-story windows and said, "Yum."

Then he added, "If—and it's a big if, Kati— if once the corbita is loaded it overnights in the lagoon, I'll consider helping. Ok?"

Katina nodded, too relieved to speak.

10. AT LAST

Katina had to wait three agonizing days before she could act. Each day, morning, noon, and night, she dashed down to the dock to check on the corbita. Each time, she would try to judge how long it would take to load the remaining cargo. There was no way of telling if the corbita would overnight in the lagoon before leaving Socotra.

Then at last, late on the afternoon of the third day, Katina got her answer. She glanced up from her after-school work on the beach, sorting freshly caught fish, and spotted the cargo ship. It was edging down the inlet, powered by its small bow sail. Halfway between the prow and the mast stood the grand figure of the owner, flanked by his soldiers.

Katina looked out to sea and the reddening sky. Yes! It was too late in the day for them to depart. It'd be far too dangerous to navigate the break in the lagoon. Their captain wouldn't be able to see well enough to pick out the edge of the coral reef or avoid the sand bars that made leaving Suq so tricky. They'd have to drop anchor in the lagoon for the night.

To the west, the sky was clear, but to the northeast, where the weather came from at this time of year, clouds were gathering. A storm would buy them time, but Katina was too much of a fisherman's daughter to wish for bad weather at sea. Fishermen died, and boats and livelihoods were wrecked when storms blew up around Socotra.

Katina turned and looked inland toward the mountains. The craggy tops were hidden by fast-moving clouds, suggesting the winds high up in the sky were much stronger than the sea breeze rustling Katina's tunic. High winds on the mountains often indicated a gathering storm, but not always.

Next she looked for Hector. He was down by his dhow, a dripping net slung in wide loops over his shoulder. He, too, was watching the corbita.

Katina crossed her fingers, hoping Hector wouldn't take too long to make up his mind. She and Hector were Asha's last chance of escape, but would he help? Would he just tell her to mind her own business? Katina knew that was what her oldest brother, Thomas, would say. Hector was different, though. He was like Mr. Dumas— generous with his help, especially during the summer monsoon when the winds were too fierce and the seas too wild to fish.

If the wind was right tomorrow morning, the corbita would leave, taking Asha and Sachin far out to sea and beyond any possible help. Tonight was their only chance of escape, and Hector was Katina's only hope.

All through dinner, Katina watched and waited for Hector to speak. He had his thinking face on. When thinking, he managed to appear as if he was looking at nothing in particular. Katina resisted the urge to restate her argument. He had to agree, he simply had to.

She barely tasted her grilled jack fish. Even her favorite dessert, rice pudding flavored with a little of Mr. Dumas's cardamom and topped with a crisp layer of seared sugar, passed her lips without comment. Katina did notice her parents exchanging an "Oh well, nothing to be done" look. They always did that when something upset Katina that they expected would pass.

It wasn't until her mother poured the coffee that Hector cleared his throat to speak. Katina held her breath. He had to agree, he simply had to.

"Papa," he said finally. "It's a full moon, so I thought I might take Kati out for a bit of night fishing in the lagoon. We won't be late."

Katina exhaled. Yes! Hector hadn't failed her. She switched her attention to her father. If he didn't agree, all would be lost.

Her father grinned at her. "Well, you look eager."

"Yes, Papa. May we please? We won't go out of the lagoon, I promise."

"You'd better not," agreed her father.

"We wouldn't dream of it, Papa," said Hector solemnly.

Her father chuckled. "All right. Katina, you're to pay attention and do as you're told. There's no better way to learn to sail and fish than by example."

Katina leapt to her feet and dashed over to give her father a hug. "Thank you, Papa. I'll be good, I promise."

Katina stood on the beach next to Hector's dhow, staring into the moonlit darkness, trying to make out the location of the corbita. The humid night was heavy with the complex scents of Socotra. The cries of nightjars and owls sounded from the date palms, and the geckos seemed to call out their own names. In front of her was the constant swish of waves lapping on the beach and the distant boom of surf on the reef.

"There she is," said Hector, pointing out across the water. "A little to the east of the break in the lagoon. Positioned for a quick getaway in the morning, I'd say."

When Katina didn't reply, he raised her hand to the sky. "See where Leo's rising? You remember the stars in the shape of a lion, don't you? Those two stars —they're the lion's jaw, Kati. The corbita's right below the eastern-most one."

Katina lowered her eyes from the stars and saw the faintest flickering of oil lamps in the distance, where normally no light would be. "Got it," she said. "Will we have to row?" She licked a finger to test the wind speed.

"Yes," said Hector. "The wind has dropped down quite a bit. It's too light to sail in. I'd rather row anyway. It makes less noise than sailing. No creaking ropes and slapping sails to give us away." He paused for a moment, leaning up against the prow of the boat.

In the moonlight, Katina saw him scratch his chin, and she crossed her fingers in the dark. Please don't change your mind now, she thought. Please don't pull out.

Hector cleared his throat. "Have you thought this through, Kati? You know the corbita's fully loaded. They have no room left below for the crew. They'll be sleeping on deck, so we won't be able to just sidle up beside the ship and throw a rope up over the rail. You never know whom we might hit."

Katina hadn't thought of that, but she wasn't giving up now. Somehow she had to keep Hector believing they could do this. "I have a plan," she said. "I know exactly how to make contact."

"Ok, but I'm not letting you climb aboard. It's too dangerous for you and the Patel kids. You've got to get them to come to us, without the crew or soldiers knowing we're there. Can you do that, Kati?"

"Yes! Once we've made contact, we'll speak Sanskrit. That way none of the Alexandrians or crew will understand us."

"I didn't know you spoke Sanskrit," said Hector.

"Asha and I speak Sanskrit together all the time." She thought it best not to tell him that Asha had taught Katina Sanskrit so they could converse in private at school, where the teacher and most of the other girls only spoke Greek.

"Can you get Asha and Sachin to come to us, Kati?"

"I'm sure I can. We have a secret signal. Asha will know it's me. I promise."

"Ok," conceded Hector, all business now. "While you organize them, I'll keep an ear on what the crew are up to. If I decide we have to get out of there, there's to be no argument. I'm just going to go. All right?"

"All right," said Katina quietly.

"Good. Well, let's go then. In you hop, Kati. Ready the oars while I push off."

Katina clambered over the side of the dhow and pulled the oars out from under the worn plank seats. She glanced up to the star to get her bearings, taking care to hold on as the dhow began to slip forward off the beach and into the sea.

Moments later, she heard Hector splashing through the shallows as he pushed the dhow further out into the water. Katina felt the boat wobble and lurch slightly as its hull left the sand behind and they began to float. She tightened her grip on the seat, waiting for the dhow to list and lurch as Hector jumped in, ready to shuffle along the seat in the opposite direction to counterbalance his weight.

The dhow found its center of gravity as soon as Hector seated himself in the center of the boat. "Keep your eyes on that star, Kati, and let me know if we veer off course," he said, settling in with his back toward the corbita and the open sea. "Tap my right knee if I need to go right—"

"And your left knee if you need to go left. Will do," Katina finished.

He took the oars Katina handed him and slipped them into the water, pulling smoothly to send the dhow gliding quietly across the lagoon. Each stroke propelled them closer to Asha. As she listened to Hector's controlled breathing and the splish of the oars, Katina kept thinking, not long now, Asha. Not long now.

11. RESCUE ATTEMPT

Voices and laughter were carried to them on the warm night air as they neared the corbita. The lagoon was choppy, but their progress was steady, and soon Katina could see the dark shape of the cargo ship, outlined in the night by an array of tiny lights on the deck.

Hector pulled up the oars. In the moonlight, Katina saw him tilt his head as he listened for the sound of the waves lapping against the hull of the corbita. It wasn't easy to hear over the boom of the surf on the reef.

The dhow began to roll as the slight swell began to build, telling Katina that bad weather was on its way. The sea always deteriorated first. A rising swell was a warning of worse to come.

"Sea's building," Hector murmured. He sounded worried. For a moment, Katina thought he'd use a single oar to turn them back toward the shore, but instead he silently slipped both oars back into the water and began to row once more, as slowly and quietly as he could.

As they got closer, snatches of conversation in Greek drifted toward them. Katina heard no hint of Sanskrit or the high-pitched tones of children's voices. She, too, listened for the lap of the waves on the hull, trying to calculate their distance from the corbita.

They were getting close. Soon they were so close that the bulk of the ship blotted out the stars. Moonlight streamed forward across the top of its deck, split by its mast into two pools of lit water. Behind the pools of light was the dark shadow cast on the water by the corbita's hull. That was where they were heading—into the safety of the shadow.

Using one oar at a time, Hector maneuvered them as close as he could until, with a gentle bump, they connected with the lowest of the corbita's wale plankings. Hector grasped at the wale as they began to bounce off, trying to pull the dhow gently alongside, but the wet wood slipped through his grasp and the swell lifted them up and away from the ship.

As Hector tried to bring the dhow in close again, Katina cupped her hands around her mouth, imitating the distinctive prrrp call of the African scops owl. She counted to five, then prrrped again. After counting to three, she repeated the call a third time.

Katina lowered her hands, listening as hard as she could. Just as she was thinking of raising her hands to repeat the sequence, she heard it— an answering call from somewhere toward the stern of the boat. She counted to five and the call sounded again. Katina concentrated and counted to three. Yes! There it was again. Asha had answered!

Just at that moment, the dhow bounced hard against the corbita's hull, and Katina froze, listening to the dull thud, frighteningly loud, echo across the lagoon. She heard Hector's sharp intake of breath. A ripple of male laughter from the stern wafted across the night air. No alarm was sounded.

Katina allowed herself to breathe again, filling her nostrils with the smoke of rancid lamp oil combined with the scent of a fried fish dinner. Suddenly, an explosive curse erupted from right above them. Hector caught Katina's arm to steady her as they listened to a crewman grumbling about a chain and hook left lying around so he could break his toe on it. Katina's blood pounded in her ears so loudly that she was sure the crewman must be able to hear it.

She took a moment to calm herself and then repeated her owl calls, hoping to guide Asha to the dhow's position beside the corbita. Then the waiting began again, but not for long. A whispered greeting in Sanskrit wafted over the rail somewhere above them. It was Asha's voice. "Katina, is that you?

"Take the oars, Kati," whispered Hector urgently, as the swell pushed them dangerously close to the corbita's hull.

Katina slid forward to grab the oars, and Hector raised his hands to fend off the corbita as it pitched and rolled above them.

"We've got to get out of here," he hissed. "The sea's getting too rough."

The words were barely out of his mouth when a wave slammed them against the ship with a hideous, wood-splintering crunch. Up on the corbita, a cry of "Pirates" rang out, accompanied by the thunder of running feet. All along the deck, the alarm was repeated and relayed.

Hector snatched the oars from Katina and had just enough time to haul on them twice, opening up a stretch of black water between the boats, before an array of torches popped up along the rail of the corbita. They freckled the sea below like lamplight through a loosely woven blanket.

"Get down," hissed Hector. "As low as you can. Quick!"

He took another furtive pull on the oars as Katina hunkered down. She heard the pinging of bowstrings being released, followed by the whiz of arrows slicing through the air. Hector dropped down beside her as an arrow whistled overhead. They could hear arrows plopping into the sea around them. There was no way to tell if they'd been spotted or if the soldiers were shooting at random into the darkness.

Katina was about to raise her head to check when an arrow thudded into the side of the dhow, twanging as it stuck fast.

"That's it," muttered Hector. Stooping as low as possible, he started rowing frantically for the shore. As they pulled away, they heard another volley of arrows taking flight, but none fell near the dhow. Katina heard someone yell that the pirates were escaping.

Then, rising above the angry shouts in Greek, Katina heard the unmistakable sound of Asha's voice, crying out in Sanskrit. "Katina, don't leave me here!"

Hector paused mid-stroke, as if he had recognized the desperation in Asha's voice, even though he hadn't understood her words. Before Katina could ask him to return, he said between heavy breaths, "Sorry, Kati. Can't risk it."

"But—"

"But nothing. It's too rough, and it's too dangerous."

"But—" Katina began again.

"There's a storm coming," Hector interrupted. "That corbita won't be going anywhere tomorrow."

Though they were now out of earshot of the corbita, Asha's cry was repeating over and over in Katina's mind. Hector was rowing like a man possessed, his breathing getting louder and more labored as they neared the shore.

In her heart, Katina knew he was right. The dhow was rocking and rolling as it crested the waves that were now racing across the lagoon. It was too dangerous, and now too rough, to try again later. Knowing that they had had no choice but to leave didn't stop Katina from feeling like a failure, though. In turning the dhow and running for shore, they'd left Asha to her fate.

The moment they hit the shallows, Hector pulled up the oars and leapt out to haul the dhow up the beach. Together they hauled the family's other two dhows up past the storm surge line. Then Hector sent Katina home while he went to warn the other fishermen to haul their boats further up the beach, out of range of the coming storm.

Later that night, Katina lay in bed, listening to the wind howl and screech. It was as if the tiny teeth of wind that had nipped her ankles on the

Sabbath had grown into fangs that tore into the date palms and gnawed at the houses. As if in competition, the sea roared and bellowed back at the wind. Squalls of rain joined the fray. Above all the noise, Katina kept hearing, again and again, Asha's mournful cry.

By first light, the storm was raging in full force. Katina crept out of bed and listened to the sleeping household. Her father and brothers only got to sleep in when it was too rough to fish.

Quietly, she dressed, tiptoed down the stairs, and opened the front door, hanging on tight when the wind tried to rip it from her grasp. Even though Katina knew no sea captain would be crazy enough to leave the lagoon in these conditions, she had to check to make sure the corbita was still there. She had to be sure she'd not botched her only chance to rescue Asha and Sachin.

Katina wrapped her cloak around her, shielding her nose and mouth from the sand-laden wind. It stung her legs and ankles, but she was determined to get down to the beach. She ducked from building to building, taking as much shelter as she could from the wild weather. It wasn't raining now, but the sky was black and threatening.

As she cleared the last of the shelter offered by the town, Katina hunched into her cloak, her eyes on the ground. Out here, the sand flew so thick the dunes seemed to be dancing, coloring the air a gritty brown. It was only when the sand rasping against her legs began to feel damp, and she could see the first of the dhows hauled high up on the beach, that Katina raised her eyes.

12. STORM

Katina was still well back from the sea, yet the wind was hurling the spray so high in the air, it carried to where she stood, spattering her cloak and face with cold water. The air was full of the salty smell of kelp rising from the tangled heaps of coral, seaweed, driftwood, and shells dumped on the beach by the frantic sea.

Out on the reef, huge plumes of white water crashed into the lagoon, where the dual forces of the swell and tide battled the howling wind. As if trying to prevent the waves from reaching the land, the wind whipped at their white crests, forcing them sideways. Close to the shore, the lagoon was a foaming frenzy.

Katina crouched down in the shelter of the nearest beached dhow, shuddering at the thought of how seasick Asha must be. Raising a hand to shield her eyes from the driving spray, she looked out across the wild water to where the corbita had been anchored.

It wasn't there!

Katina peered around the stern of the dhow and froze. The ship had broken free of its sea anchor and was being driven toward the beach, slewing from side to side as each wave caught it and washed over its deck.

Katina leapt to her feet and ran. She had to raise the alarm. She had to ring the shipwreck bell, alert the town. Every moment lost could cost a life. Her sandals snagged, tripping her nose-first into the sand, but she scrambled to her feet and kept running, without pausing to dust off her clothes and face.

At last she reached the edge of the town where the old Chinese bell hung. Her cold hands slipped on the rope that secured the wooden log suspended beside the bronze bell.

"Come on, come on, come on," muttered Katina as she unwound the rope and, with a mighty heave, started ringing the huge bell. The deafening sound even drowned out the roaring wind and surf, waking all of Suq.

With each ear-shattering peel, Katina's head felt as if it would explode, but she continued to heave on the rope to keep it ringing. She was so deafened by the bell that she didn't hear Mr. Dumas approach.

While he took over the ringing duties at twice the speed Katina could manage, she dashed to the nearest house and helped the women and children carry blankets down to the beach. Up ahead, Katina could see Mr. Patel and the other men assembling rescue ropes and splitting into teams to haul survivors from the sea.

Out on the lagoon, the corbita was being thrown around like a toy. It was listing dangerously—a sure sign that its cargo had moved or, worse still, that it was taking on water. Peering through the spray, Katina thought she could make out arms waving on the deck and more still thrashing in the sea.

A team of men advanced into the shallows, helping Hector and Thomas launch Thomas' dhow. Such was the force of the sea, even two of Suq's strongest men rowing together would have to struggle to make any headway at all.

Two other teams of men fed out ropes attached to pearl divers, the best swimmers in Suq. Every child in Suq was taught that, when the sea foamed, swimmers sank, so only the most powerful swimmers could attempt rescues in these conditions. The divers waded into the shallows and dove into the churning waves.

Katina didn't know where to look—at her brothers' dhow lurching across the lagoon, at the pearl divers, visible one moment and gone the next, or at the corbita. She didn't dare think about Asha. Someone tapped her shoulder and put a rope in her hands as the women added their pulling power to the rescue teams.

As a second dhow was launched, the rope in Katina's hands went taut. She hung on. Then, in unison, the team hauled, taking one backward step after another, dragging their pearl diver, and the survivor he'd rescued, from the waves.

It took all of Katina's concentration to keep her footing and pull her share of the weight. The slightest stumble would send a ripple effect all along the rope that could cost a life. Katina no longer noticed her saturated clothes sticking to her sandy legs. Over and over, her team dragged people from the water and then returned to rob the sea of another victim.

Up and down the beach, the inhabitants of Suq worked as one. The older women swarmed around the survivors, wrapping them in blankets and hustling them away from the rescue effort. Once safe in nearby houses, they were warmed with hot food; the dead were dealt with by the older men.

All the while, Mr. Dumas kept the shipwreck bell ringing. Its call for help echoed off the mountains, bringing aid from near and far.

Katina's team was walking forward again, ready to launch another roped swimmer into the water. As they paused, Katina's eyes sought out her brothers' dhow. She prayed that they, too, wouldn't perish. All the rescuers in and on the water were risking their lives.

At last she spotted Thomas' dhow beside the corbita. The stricken ship was close to the shore now but still in water deeper than the tallest Socotran. Katina thought she could make out people slithering down the hull of the corbita into the dhow, but the spray and wind made it hard to see clearly.

Katina concentrated on her task. Her arms and legs were aching. Her hands were raw, and still they were pulling people from the water. As the dhows approached the beach, the teams broke up and re-formed with the strongest of the men wading into the shallows to help pull the dhows up onto the beach. Katina saw Unice's brother Nate in line behind her father, waist-deep in the water.

Again, Katina took her share of the weight. This time she could see the fishing boats nearing the safety of the shore. Soon she'd be able to see who they had managed to rescue. Katina didn't dare think about Asha or Sachin. She just concentrated on her footing and hauled as hard as she could.

The moment the dhows were safe, the rope in Katina's hands went slack, but still she hung back as the others flocked around the boats. She desperately wanted to see Asha being helped out onto the sand, but she couldn't bear to look. What if Asha hadn't made it? By the inlet, a line of bodies lay covered in sacking. What if Asha was among them?

To her amazement, Katina saw that her palms were bleeding where the rope had grazed away the skin. She hadn't even noticed. She was still staring at her hands when Hector yelled in her ear. "Guess who I've got here, Kati."

As Katina whirled around, Asha flung her arms around her neck, sodden and cold. She had kelp tangled in her dripping hair and smelt like a fish, but she was safe. Soon an equally bedraggled Sachin was standing beside them, carrying a bawling little boy in his arms.

Before Katina and Asha could do anything but laugh and cry, an elated scream sounded from further up the beach. Moments later, they were enveloped by Mrs. Patel and Asha's many sisters.

As they were bundled off to a neighboring house, everyone talked at once, but it wasn't until they were inside and away from the noise of the storm that Katina could hear much of what was being said.

The teacher was overseeing the serving of the hot food. Rubbed down and wrapped in warm blankets, Katina and Asha sat arm and arm, drinking Leia's hot soup, while Mrs. Patel and Mrs. Nepos fussed over the little boy and dried his tears. It was only then that Katina realized that the frightened little boy was the son of the lord of the corbita. She hadn't recognized him without his airs and graces. There was no sign of his father or sister.

When Katina asked Asha if she'd seen them, she shook her head. "I was so seasick late last night that I was sent out on deck," Asha said. "I haven't seen them since before sunrise. They weren't on deck when I was washed overboard. I hope they were on another dhow."

Her worried frown lifted, and she beamed at Katina. "I knew you wouldn't abandon me," said Asha. "I just knew it. They didn't guess last night that you were trying to rescue me. I was so worried that you might have been hit by arrows. You weren't, were you?"

"One hit Hector's dhow, but not us." A wave of tiredness swept over Katina. She had hardly slept at all last night, and now Asha and Sachin were safe.

The house had filled up with survivors and rescuers, all exhausted by their ordeal, and neither Katina nor Asha noticed Unice standing alone in a corner of the crowded room.

13. REWARD

The next morning dawned clear and quiet. Katina hurried through her chores and then asked if she could pick up Asha early for school. "Sit down, Katina," said her mother, patting the chair beside her.

Something about her mother's quiet tone made the hairs on the back of Katina's neck prickle, but she sat obediently and listened. "After lunch, I think you should go and pick up Unice for school. She's your friend, too. Don't forget how she took care of you this last week."

Katina opened her mouth to protest, but her mother held up a hand. "Asha won't be going to school," she said. "As soon as the corbita is refloated and reloaded, she'll be going to Alexandria."

Katina felt a chill run through her. She couldn't believe her ears. They'd rescued Asha. How could it be that nothing had changed? It didn't make sense.

"The Patels have a contract, Katina," her mother continued. "Mr. Patel is a trader, and there's no way a good trader will break a contract. Now, go and brush your hair. The lord of the corbita wants to address the town at midday, and I don't want you looking like a stray cat."

Katina did as she was told in a daze. Yesterday she had thought their troubles were over. Asha was safe. Sachin was safe. Her brothers and their friends hadn't perished in the rescue. Everything was good. How could nothing have changed? It didn't make sense.

A large crowd had gathered on the beach where the debris of yesterday's storm was still scattered across the sand. Katina could see no sign of Asha or her family. While the crowd waited for the lord of the corbita to appear, they watched a team of bulls and two dhows working to pull the merchant vessel free of the sand bar.

The bulls stood flank-deep in the calm water. At a signal from the seaward dhow, the bull driver cried "Hup," and the crowd held their breath. The bulls leaned into their yokes and began to edge forward as the corbita creaked and groaned in protest. Its bow sail filled with wind, but the corbita didn't budge.

The bull driver halted his team, and after a rest and an exchange of signals with the dhows, they tried again. At last, the corbita began to creep forward.

The bull driver dropped back to the last pair of his bulls.

"Why is he doing that?" Katina wondered out loud.

Mr. Dumas answered from behind her. "It's so he can unhitch the team if the corbita comes off too fast. Better to be safe than sorry."

Little by little, the corbita began to come free, still groaning and creaking. Neither the noise nor the waves seemed to bother the bulls, and the dhows worked with them to steer the corbita when it finally floated free. As the bull driver unhitched the team, the ship deployed its steering oars, and the breeze took over the work. The crowd cheered and clapped as the bulls ambled out of the water, but Katina didn't feel like joining in.

The lord of the corbita stepped out in front of the townsfolk of Suq, flanked by his children and Asha and Sachin. It was the first time Katina had seen the lord without his soldiers. Asha was ashen-faced, but Sachin stood tall with his hands behind his back. Katina glanced over her shoulder and saw the Patels. Mrs. Patel's eyes were red and puffy.

After a silence for those who had died in the storm, the lord of the corbita raised his head. "I wish to thank each and every one of you," he said in a commanding voice. "Without the bravery and teamwork of this town, my crew, family, and ship would have perished." He paused for a moment before going on. "Later today, my soldiers will visit every home in Suq. They will present the head of each household with a token of my thanks." Sachin stepped forward holding open the neck of a large canvas bag.

Awestruck murmurs rippled through the crowd when the lord of the corbita lifted a handful of precious Socotran pearls from the bag. They shone like stars in the daylight as he held them aloft. "One pearl will be given to each household with my thanks."

Whispers of surprise and joy were echoing around Katina. Few families in Suq could afford anything as valuable as a pearl. Those few with money could keep the a pearl as a keepsake; those with less money could sell theirs to the traders at the port.

The lord of the corbita waited until the buzz died down, and then he signaled to Mr. Dumas to step forward. Apparently startled at being singled out, he bobbed his head and stepped from one foot to the other and back again.

"I have reserved my special thanks for Mr. Dumas," continued the lord of the corbita, "as he is the one who raised the alarm—"

"Oh no, no, no," interrupted Mr. Dumas, waving a hand, his head bobbing more vigorously than ever. "It was not me. It was young Katina Alexis who raised the alarm and woke the town."

The lord of the corbita raised his eyebrows. Asha clapped her hands for a moment, but an elbow in the ribs from Sachin silenced her.

Mr. Dumas propelled Katina forward. "This is Katina Alexis, sir. She raised the alarm."

Katina looked at her toes. She didn't want to look at him. This was the man who had ignored her on the street, the man who was taking Asha away.

The lord of the corbita held out his hand, and Katina looked at it. She wanted to turn her back on him, but she knew better. At last, still looking at her toes, Katina shook his hand. It was smooth and warm, not hardened by years of hard work like her father's hands.

"Thank you, Katina Alexis," said the lord of the corbita.

"You're welcome," replied Katina in a very low voice.

"Please tell me what you would like as your reward. Don't be shy."

Katina looked up and was surprised to see kindness in the powerful man's brown eyes. She looked across at Asha, bit her lip, and then said in a rush, "Please let Asha and Sachin stay. Please don't make them leave. Sachin can work for my brother fishing, and Asha could go back to school. I know they've signed a contract but . . ."

Katina trailed off as her courage deserted her. She would have turned and fled if Mr. Dumas hadn't patted her shoulder.

"Wouldn't you rather have pearls or coin?" asked the lord of the corbita. "Pretty jewelry, perhaps?"

Katina shook her head. She knew if she tried to speak her voice would tremble. Worse still, Sachin was glaring at her. She didn't dare look at Asha. She didn't want to start crying, not with everyone watching.

"I see," said the lord of the corbita. He turned to Sachin. "What have you to say, young man?"

Sachin cleared his throat. "Sir, I wish to be a scribe. I cannot do that on Socotra. Here I can only work as a fisherman's boy. Your contract offers me a future I could only dream of here. I would be honored to fulfill my contract."

Katina's heart sank, but now the lord of the corbita turned to Asha. "What about you, Asha Patel. What would you prefer to do?"

Katina raised her eyes just high enough to see Asha's face. She'd never known Asha to be short of courage, and Asha didn't fail her. She straightened her shoulders and said, "I wish to stay here and go to school, but my parents can't afford to keep me at school, sir."

"You want to stay?"

"Yes, sir," answered Asha in a clear, strong voice.

The lord of the corbita inclined his head and held a whispered conversation with Mr. Dumas. No one in the crowd spoke. It was as if everyone was holding their breath. At last, he nodded and held out his hands. "Very well, Katina Alexis. Your request is unusual, but I shall grant it. Asha Patel,

I release you from your contract. Mr. Dumas will make arrangements with your parents for you to stay in school."

Then he turned and departed, followed by his children.

Asha leapt for joy as the townsfolk cheered. She hugged Katina and then dashed over to her mother and sisters.

"You could have thought of your family instead of just yourself," said Thomas quietly, with a nudge at Katina's ribs. "We could have been rich if you'd used your brains."

"Nonsense," said Hector. "He couldn't have given us riches and not given them to everyone else. Think about it, Thomas. Good for you for speaking your mind, Kati."

Mr. Dumas bobbed his agreement. "Don't be late for school, young Kati. We don't want the teacher flying into a rage, do we?"

Katina shook her head, still not trusting herself to speak. She looked around. Most people were heading off to take care of their afternoon's business. Mrs. Patel was hugging Asha. Mr. Patel was shaking Sachin's hand and patting him on the back, the way he did with the other traders. Unice stood alone off to one side, twisting her hands together.

Katina remembered her mother's words and waved. "Unice!" she shouted.

Unice looked from Katina to Asha without moving nearer, so Katina went over to her and linked arms. "Coming to school?" she asked.

Unice bit her lip but didn't reply.

"Sorry I didn't talk to you yesterday after the rescue," said Katina. "I was just so worried that Asha and my brothers might drown. When I found out they were all right, I just sort of stopped thinking. Are you still my friend?"

"What about Asha?" asked Unice in a small voice.

"Asha likes you, too. The three of us can be best friends, can't we?"

The silver trail of a tear ran down the side of Unice's nose. She wiped it away with the back of her hand and nodded as Asha bounced over and put her arms around their shoulders. "Papa said I can spend half my pay from my last week's work. We can go to the market after school and split it three ways between us."

Unice smiled. "We'd better not be late for school then."

Glossary

abacus
An ancient calculator. People used it to do math by sliding counters along rods or in grooves.

African scops owl
A small owl found throughout sub-Saharan Africa and surrounding areas. It has a distinctive prrrp call that is repeated around every five seconds.

aloe
A succulent plant with spikes of vibrant flowers and large, fleshy leaves.

amphora
An ancient jar or jug with two handles and a narrow neck. It was often used to hold liquids such as oil or wine.

bagla	Traditional Indian sea-going vessel, or dhow. Often built from teak, they have carried foreign trade goods to and from Indian ports during the last two thousand years.
Barbary falcon	A medium-sized falcon with yellow-rimmed eyes. It lives in semi-desert areas and around dry, open hills.
Bedouin	Tribal desert-dwelling nomads of Arabia, the Negev, and the Sinai.
Byzantine Empire	Often called the Eastern Roman Empire; centered around the city of Byzantium.
Byzantium	An ancient city that stood where the modern city of Istanbul now stands.

corbita	A Roman cargo ship powered by sail, with steering oars toward the back of the boat on each side of the hull. Larger corbitas could have two or three masts.
dhow	A boat with a triangular sail. The boat was made by sewing the hull boards together with woven fiber, cords, or thongs.
dowry/ dowries	The money or property given by a bride's family to her husband at marriage.
dragon's blood tree	An unusual tree native to Socotra. It is the source of the highly valued dragon's blood resin, which is used for dyes and medicinal purposes.
egret	A type of white heron that has long plumes during the breeding season.

ghee   Butter that is heated until the milk solids separate and the remaining liquid butter is clear. It is often used in Indian cooking.

laughing dove   A long-tailed, slim pigeon.

markab   A sea-going, double-ended dhow with steering oars at the stern and a four-sided sail.

osprey   A large hawk that feeds on fish. It is sometimes called a sea hawk.

prow   Another name for the front part of a vessel.

Sabbath   A day of rest and worship.

saffron   An expensive, yellow-colored flavoring that comes from the crocus flower.